GREG the SAUSAGE ROLL

THE PERFECT PRESENT

To Phoenix and Kobe,
never give up on your dreams.
Love Mum and Dad xx – R. H. and M. H.

For Katie and Megan, the (fairy) lights of my life x – G. C.

PUFFIN BOOKS

UK | USA | Canada | Ireland | Australia | India | New Zealand | South Africa

Puffin Books is part of the Penguin Random House group of companies whose addresses can be found at global.penguinrandomhouse.com

www.penguin.co.uk   www.puffin.co.uk   www.ladybird.co.uk

Penguin
Random House
UK

First published 2022

001

Text and illustrations copyright © Mark and Roxanne Hoyle, 2022
Illustrations by Gareth Conway

The moral right of the authors has been asserted.
"It's Beginning to Look a Lot Like Christmas" copyright © Meredith Wilson, 1951
"Shivers" written by Ed Sheeran, Johnny McDaid, Steve Mac and Kal Lavelle, ℗ & © 2021 Warner Music UK Limited
"2step" written by Ed Sheeran, Andrew Watt, Louis Bell and David Hodges, ℗ & © 2021 Warner Music UK Limited

Printed and bound in Italy

The authorized representative in the EEA is Penguin Random House Ireland, Morrison Chambers, 32 Nassau Street, Dublin D02 YH68

A CIP catalogue record for this book is available from the British Library

ISBN: 978-0-241-54835-6

All correspondence to: Puffin Books, Penguin Random House Children's, One Embassy Gardens, 8 Viaduct Gardens, London SW11 7BW

MIX
Paper from
responsible sources
FSC® C018179

GREG the SAUSAGE ROLL

THE PERFECT PRESENT

MARK AND ROXANNE HOYLE

Illustrated by Gareth Conway

PUFFIN

"CHRISTMAAAAAAASS!"

Greg exclaimed.

"YES, MAAAAAATE!" cried Frosty and Yules.

Greg jumped on to the counter and took a deep breath. "At last!
It's time for me to go-ho-ho on a VERY special mission," he announced.

And, with that, Greg was off!

"Where are you going, Greg?!" called Gloria.

"Wait and seeeeeeeeee!" he shouted with a cheeky grin.

Out on the busy street,
Greg spotted three French hens . . .

Bonjour!

Coooeeeee!!

two turtle doves . . .

and a post box by a pear tree.

"GET INNNN . . . !" whooped Greg
as he ran towards it.

"Almost . . . there!" puffed Greg.

"I DID IT!" Greg cheered. "And now to make SURE I arrive on time . . ." He slapped on a stamp, tied on a tag and eagerly waited for the postie to collect him.

In no time at all, Greg found himself at the post office. He had never seen anything like it! He spotted a HUGE sparkly postbag and he squealed with joy.

NORTH POLE

To Fatha chrismus

Santaclaws lapland

To F.C. Reindeerland North

"CANNONBAAALLL!"

Now he was only a hop, skip and a jump away from reaching the best place ever . . .

Before long, Greg had made it. "I'm at Santa's house - in the NORTH POLE!" he cheered.

With a shiver of excitement, Greg pushed the door open and looked inside . . .

"WOW" said Greg, beaming. "Now, I wonder which door leads to Santa?!
I'm a sausage roll on a mission . . ."

First, Greg peered round the door marked . . .

Next, he stuck his head round the door labelled . . .

Greg tried the next door, called 'WRAP STARS'...

"OH MY CHRISTMAS JUMPERS!"
cried Greg. "This is the best day of
my whole life!!!"

Greg couldn't wait to test out all the toys – IMMEDIATELY!

First, he attempted some sick skating tricks.

Next, he tried to be the world's best gamer and reach Boss Level.

Then he tested every colour of fidget spinner – round and round and round!

And he even checked out the latest animal filters.

As Greg continued to explore, he heard a loud sniff and looked up to discover a very friendly-looking elf. He waved at him. "Hello! I'm Greg!"
"Hey there, Greg! I thought I could smell something delicious that gives me the shivers! I'm Elf Sheeran, Chief Elf. What brings you here?"

"I'm here to see my friend Santa. Do you know where he is?" Greg asked.
"Santa is VERY busy at the moment," said Elf Sheeran.
"Oh dear," said the little sausage roll. His bottom lip started to tremble.

"You know, Greg, we're running a bit behind and it's our busiest night – can you help?" asked Elf Sheeran as he handed Greg an apron, hat and paintbrush. Greg nodded happily.

"LET'S TWO-STEP TO IT!" sang Elf Sheeran

Eventually, Greg stood back
to admire his hard work.
"Sausage-roll baubles? CHECK!
Puff-pastry disco balls? CHECK!"

If only Santa could see how helpful he'd been!
But where on earth *was* Santa?
Just at that moment, Chief Elf Sheeran rocked up. He took a
look at Greg's handiwork. "Well . . . thank you, Greg," he said.
"I think it's time to show you where the real magic happens.
Follow me!" And off they scarpered.

"Wow!" said Greg. "I'm just in time! I'm here to find my sausage-roll sweetheart Gloria the PERFECT PRESENT! Please, please can you help me, Santa?"
"How thoughtful, Greg!" said Santa. " Of course, I know just the gift.
I'll meet you outside in a jiffy."

A - E

F - S

T - Z

23 24

Outside, Greg waited for Santa in the crisp,
glistening snow. He couldn't resist . . .
"SAUSAGE-ROLL ANGELS!" he cried,
happily waving his arms and legs and not caring
for a moment about his soggy bottom.

Soon Santa was ready and the reindeers prepared for lift-off.
"Now, I believe THIS is what you've been searching for,"
said Santa kindly. Greg's face lit up brighter than the North Star.
'Oh, thank you, Santa,' he replied.

And with the beautifully wrapped gift safe by his side, Greg waved goodbye
to Elf Sheeran and all his elf friends, as the sleigh soared into the night.

Greg gasped in wonder as
they flew higher and **higher**
and HIGHER...

At last, they arrived back at the bakery.
"I LOVE YOU SO MUCH, SANTA – MERRY CHRISTMAAAAAS!"
called Greg, as Santa and the reindeers waved goodbye.

"Greg, you're home!" exclaimed Gloria.

"Merry Christmas!" Greg beamed, handing Gloria her present.

"Please, pleeeaaase can you open it RIGHT now? I just can't wait until tomorrow!"

"SAUSAGE ROLLER-SKATES!" cried Gloria. "Thank you, Greg!"

But Greg wasn't the only one who had planned something special. "I know how much you love Christmas, Greg," Gloria began, "so I've invited ALL your family and friends to celebrate . . ."

"SURPRIIIISE!"
Greg jumped a mile in the air.
"LOOK, Gloria! It's the whole pack!"
he said, clapping his hands in glee.

SURPRISE

SNOWM

"There's Goldie,
and Gracie,
and Gemma, and Gwen.
There's Gurdeep, Greta.
Georgie and Glen.

MINCE PIES

And Gail, Gareth,
Guy, Gus and Gabby.

There's Gina, Gabriel, Grant, Grey,
Gita, Gordon and Gary!"

"Come on, everyone,"
cheered Gloria.
"Let's PARTY!"

"Everyone say, 'SAUSAGES!'"
cried Greg as they huddled in closely. "All of us together at Christmas . . .
now THIS is the perfect present!"